VOICES OF
OUR CHILDREN
A POETRY ANTHOLOGY

Edited by
jennifer lyn amon, HEAL Program Director
Sylvie Middleton, Poetry Workshop Creator

With the children of the HEAL Community Service Program
A program of Homes with Hope, Inc.

CHRISTMAS LAKE PRESS

Published by Christmas Lake Press 2024
www.christmaslakecreative.com
Copyright 2024 Christmas Lake Press
ISBN: 978-1-960865-19-9

Interior layout by Daiana Marchesi

VOICES OF
OUR CHILDREN

A POETRY ANTHOLOGY

Dedication

This collection of poems is dedicated to the voices of our children, and to all those who were once children.

Acknowledgments

All the students who participated
from Bridgeport, Norwalk, Westport, and Wilton Schools
Lynn Abramson
Cheryl Samodel
Nancy Lewis
Brianna Andrade
Karianna Montalvo
Asia Stewart
Trinity Haswell
Thomas Fiffer and Julia Bobkoff, Christmas Lake Press
Travis Bell, Verso Studios, Recording Studios Manager,
The Westport Library
A special thank you to the Sexauer Foundation, a financial
supporter of HEAL since the beginning.

Contents

Foreword

In the early months of 2022, Homes with Hope, Inc. Vice President Paris Looney and I were meeting per the usual…speaking out loud, inspired by the HEAL students, wanting to bring positive messages to the masses. "What if, we had an icon on our website that when you clicked on it, there were audio clips of some of our students reading motivational poems, by others or, written by them!"… YES…Voices of Our Children was born. It seemed a lovely effort, but we were ill-prepared. The student members of the HEAL Community Service Program were all in when we presented the idea, but we failed to get further than sharing some of our favorite poems with only each other.

Over the summer a volunteer presented herself to Homes with Hope, wanting to help in almost any way. She was directed to our Youth Services Programs, and upon meeting poet Sylvie Middleton, we could sense something special was on the horizon.

Lynn Abramson, the Director of Homes with Hopes ASAP program, and I met with Sylvie one summer day, and we discussed our programs and opportunities for her involvement. When she spoke of being a poet, I brought up the "Voices of our Children" idea that we'd conceived a few months prior. All eyes lit up. Sylvie asked what the parameters were, and hence put together the eight-session poetry workshop that evolved into the book you are holding today.

The sessions were distinguished by different forms of poetry, all with the intent of promoting self-expression and pathways to healing. Through written word and sharing, we became seekers of hope, bringers of gifts...catalysts of change.

All submissions were written by HEAL members and leaders, ages ranging from five to sixty-five. This collective effort brought us all so much joy, and we are thrilled to be able to share our "Voices" with you!

jennifer lyn amon
HEAL Program Director

Prologue

Voices of Our Children is a compilation of poetry written by students attending Bridgeport, Norwalk, Westport, and Wilton Schools. The poems in this anthology were organized in the order that the sessions were held. The different types of poetry used in each of the sessions were intended to evoke self-awareness, trust, and a path to healing. All writing is a process of discovery, and especially poetry. Its very form allowed the students to let go of preconceived beliefs and ways of thinking. It opened up a space for them to express how they felt about giving, their favorite foods, colors, nature through Japanese haiku and "where they're from," to name a few. It was an honor and a privilege to work with these students and to witness how poetry inspired them. Knowing that writing evoked such emotions within them gives us hope that they now have a new pathway to healing.

These poems are for you, to listen and to hear the voices of our children. May you be moved and inspired by their words and authenticity.

Sylvie Middleton, Poetry Workshop Creator

Lost

Lost as a child abandoned,
confused as a youth can be,
shields worn around her gentle soul,
she wandered aimlessly.
Until the child within
held the grown woman's hand,
Until she reached inside
and found truth again.
Now it can begin, healing,
and still it all leads to you.

— *Sylvie Middleton*

Art by Jae

ONE

When Giving is All We Have
— Alberto Ríos

We opened the poetry workshop with this poem to explore the healing power of giving. The intention was for students to realize that giving is about more than providing food and shelter or volunteering. When we give through writing and we share our journeys in life, we begin to heal ourselves and others; exploring and showing that no matter how different we may seem, we all have shared expressions and experiences.

1.

I gave my friend 3 cookies
My friend gave me a hug,
Together we made butterflies.

2.

I gave my time teaching the kids
They gave me their gratitude,
Together we made each other smile.

3.

I gave my voice to those with none
The masses gave me energy pure and bright,
Together we made hope.

4.

I gave him belly-rubs and a lot of love
Jonesy gave me a lot of love,
Somebody who I can trust and tell all my secrets to,
Together we made two best friends.

5.

I gave you too much
You never gave me enough,
Together we formed something raw and broken.

6.

I gave you yin
You gave me yang,
Together we made life.

7.

You gave me music in the breeze to dance to,
a spotlight from above to guide.
I give you my attention and movement,
together we are wonderment.

8.

I gave but I never got
I think but never speak
I observe and stay hidden
I speak when spoken to.
You hate, I hate
You talk shit but I stay silent.
See, it's not always genuine…
I give because I love,
you give because you want.
I came to you with my heart,
But you took it and ripped it apart.

9.

I gave you my time, effort and trust
All you gave me was your back,
Together we made nothing but just memories.

10.

You made me feel when you put your toes in the
sand, or when there's a breeze when it's hot.
You made me feel complete
Like a bee getting pollen from a flower.

11.

I gave my cousin a hug when our uncle died
My cousin gave me a hug back
Together we made it be happy.

12.

I gave my heart, you took my shit and ran with it.
You gave me pain and heartache,
Together we made a misunderstood and broken family.

13.

I gave you my time and effort in saying good morning,
You gave me a good morning
Together, we made a good morning.

14.

I come in with my whole heart.
If you don't have any to bring,
at least to come is a start.

As long as you care, as long as you're here,
I'm more than happy to share.
I'd give you half, when you make me laugh.
Since I couldn't give you all of mine, but
that's just fine.

$0+1=1$, but so does $\frac{1}{2} + \frac{1}{2}$.
So you take the right, I'll keep the left,
As long as it's you and me, I'll still feel
whole, all by myself.

15.

I gave you the power to believe in yourself
You gave me the freedom to be myself,
Our souls sighed in relief.
This is what it means to be in love.

TWO

I Am
— John Clare

The "I Am" poem encourages self-reflection through a series of prompts inviting the students to be curious and creative about who they are. Their hopes, wishes, dreams, worries, and home truths came to light. Sharing their poems with their peers was a meaningful way to connect with each other and reveal the magic that makes each of them unique.

16.

I am nice and helpful
I wonder if I can get 2 baby turtles for my birthday
I hear teachers talking
I see the sky
I want a robot that can clean my room
I am nice and helpful.

I pretend that I fly an airplane
I feel happy
I touch the sky
I worry about heights actually
I cry if a turtle dies
I am nice and helpful.

I understand I have a fish named Uno
I say a baby turtle won't die
I dream about peeps
I try to be kind to all animals
I hope every animal in the galaxy doesn't die
I am nice and helpful.

17.

I am a mirrorball
I wonder if others can see that
I hear the laughter around me and I want to laugh
I see their love just out of reach
I want some grilled cheese
I am a mirrorball.

I pretend not to hear her despicable words
I feel heavy
I touch myself to make sure I'm still there
I worry
I cry over the empty feeling
I am a mirrorball.

I understand I need to shine for them
I say I'm okay
I dream of the wind in my hair as I leave
I try to laugh but it comes out hollow
I hope they can see I'm trying
I am a mirrorball.

18.

I am witty and unpredictable
I wonder what it's like to skydive
I hear the wind
I see the sky
I want to be free
I am witty and unpredictable.

I pretend that everything is ok as I free fall
I feel no one can hurt me
I touch peace
I worry about the future
I cry for the losses in my life
I am witty and unpredictable.

I understand the way things are
I say it's ok
I dream of a life beyond
I try to accept reality
I hope for love's recovery
I am witty and unpredictable.

19.

I am a beautiful imperfection
I wonder what more there is to life
I hear a calling from beyond
I see a path not created by me
I want to be filled with the energy from that space
I am a beautiful imperfection.

I pretend to be happy in my skin
I feel galactic exhaustion
I touch a shooting star
I worry that I cannot hang on
I cry about not being enough
I am a beautiful imperfection.

I understand it is all not on me
I say there is beauty in silence
I dream of silence
I try to be the difference
I hope my presence makes a difference
I am a beautiful imperfection.

20.

I am that Bitch that will go down in vain
I wonder how it feels to be happy
I hear the rumors and lies
I see the haters and bums
I want the money without fame
I am that bitch that will go down in vain.

I pretend to feel loved
I feel unhappy
I touch their hearts
I worry about nothing
I cry for something.

I understand music
I say I'm through with it
I dream I can do it
I try to put my foot into it
I hope to find peace all alone
I am that bitch that will go down in vain.

21.

I am who I am
I wonder why I am always mad
I hear loud and breaking up voices in my head
I see people are not always going to be there
I want to improve on myself
I am who I am.

I pretend to be happy and make sure I'm not seen down
I feel like I don't fit in with everybody
I touch people's hearts and show love
I worry that I'm not good enough
I cry when I'm not aware
I am who I am.

I understand that not everyone is going to stay
I say I am okay, but I'm not
I dream that everything would be better
I try to be okay
I hope that I can heal 100%
I am who I am.

22.

I am N.A
I wonder how many bees there are in the world
I hear music all day
I see food every day
I want food every day
I am N.A

I pretend I am indifferent
I feel I am more
I touch the hearts of others
I worry of my self-sabotage
I cry disclosed
I am N.A

I understand only what I can control
I say things that could take a toll
I dream to escape
I try for myself
I hope I am more than I imagine
I am N.A

23.

I am rare and delicate
I wonder why I'm like this
I hear the music that brings me joy
I see people hiding their pain
I want to feel different than I do
I am rare and delicate.

I pretend my problems don't exist
I feel so much pain
I touch my ferret's fur as I cry into my pillow
I worry I will never get better
I cry because I want to be normal
I am rare and delicate.

I understand that healing takes time
I say that I'm ok
I dream of telling the truth
I try to heal from the pain they caused
I hope I get better
I am rare and delicate.

24.

I am depressed but I will be ok
I wonder what it's like to be happy
I hear what they say
I see what they do
I want freedom and happiness
I am depressed but I will be ok.

I pretend I'm doing just fine
I feel broken inside
I touch their hearts
I worry because I care
I cry because I'm dying inside
I am depressed but I will be ok.

I understand they are trying to help
I say "I'm ok"
I dream it will be over soon
I try not to think because it hurts
I hope it will all blow over
I am depressed but I will be ok.

25.

I am a part of everything and everyone
I wonder how it would feel to bear what
I hear from all the happy and sad lives around me
I see everywhere with thoughtful eyes from my back to my
front
I want to do everything that I can be
I am a part of everything and everyone.

I pretend that my deepest dreams are real
I feel so little but I feel so much
I touch hearts that break fast and hurried
I worry that as hard as I try, I'll never know why?
I cry at everything because I'm just human
I am a part of everything and everyone.

I understand very little, but I try and I pray
I say words kind, of the mind, and never words mean
I dream my family and friends will always be fine
I try to kill the negativity and find ways to cope
I hope that I can live up to my plan
I am a part of everything and everyone.

26.

I am a girl with brown hair
I wonder what job I will have
I hear money $$$$
I see money $$$$
I want money $$$$
I am a girl with brown hair.

I pretend I have 20 dollars $$$$
I feel Benjamin Franklins in my pockets
I touch money $$$$
I worry I won't have money $$$$
I cry when I have no money $$$$
I am a girl with brown hair.

I understand it will be hard to make money
I say Cha-Ching Cha-Ching $$$$
I dream for money
I try making money
I hope I get money
I am a girl with brown hair.

THREE

Let's Do Haiku

Haiku is a form of poetry that began in thirteenth-century Japan and uses the senses to describe scenes from nature. In this session the goal was to awaken the students to the possibility of finding poetry and meaning in the natural world around them and how they relate to it.

27.

The Last Day of Summer

Summer slips far away
Sweet crisp air kisses her cheek,
Misery follows.

28.

Water

Water is soothing
Water is a tsunami
Water is like life.

29.

Snowflake

Here comes the snowflake
Unique, glittering, perfect
Pop! Melts on my tongue.

30.

Yesterday

Don't cry, don't cry dear
the sun has risen today
Yesterday is gone.

31.

Flowers

Some flowers are dead
Some are life-like flowers but,
None are pretty like you.

32.

Pillow, car beam, one marshmallow,
teddy bear,
care teddy bears are cute.

33.

Loud Morning

It's early morning
The only sound I hear outside now
are my peckish birds

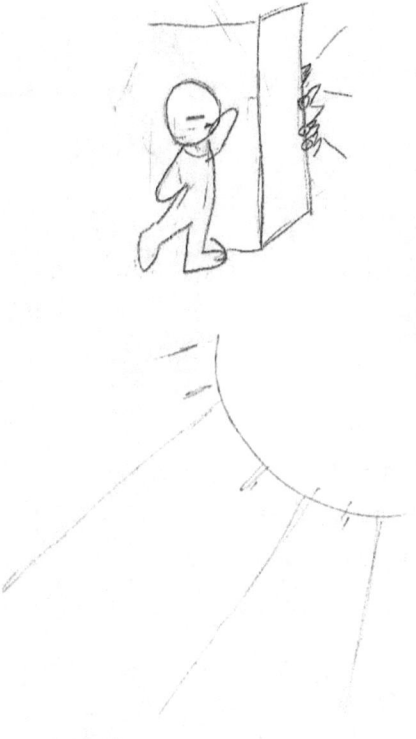

34.

Sun whispers warm thoughts
Exhilarating message
Its rays feed my soul.

35.

Baby cat follows
She knows where to find cuddles
and the warm, warm sun.

36.

My Mental

Weight on my shoulders
I know somewhere I'll find peace
Watch me burn for love.

37.

Autumn's Breath

Fading leaves like fall
Whispered beauty turns to gray,
Autumn's lonely end.
Lonely leaves that fall,
embracing their final rest.
Autumn's mournful sigh.

38.

Renewal

Sun sets, blushing pink
Ending yet another day
But we'll start anew.

39.

Twilight

Between day and night
Breath held, ready to let go
Fall into the dusk.

FOUR

Five Senses Color Poem

Colors influence our lives and can evoke different emotions and memories that may want to surface. In this session students were asked to think about colors, while imagining what these colors taste, feel, smell, sound, and look like. The intention was to create an outlet where they could experience how colors directly influence reactions to their environments.

40.

Grey

Grey looks like school days
Grey sounds like alarms in the morning
Grey smells like newly burnt wood ashes
Grey tastes like melted vanilla ice cream on a sad snowy day
Grey feels like the first month of school
Grey reminds me of the end of the weekend.

41.

Red

Red looks like a watermelon
Red sounds like an angry song
Red smells like flowers
Red tastes like strawberries
Red feels like bumpy
Red reminds me of an angry face.

42.

Red

Red looks like a heart
Red sounds like people without a breath
Red smells like strawberries
Red tastes like a pizza
Red feels like a lot of energy
Red reminds me of lips.

43.

Colors, a collection

Roses are red, violets are blue
Flowers are beautiful, but not as beautiful as you.

Roses are red, violets are blue
Rhymes may not rhyme, but we will fix that.

Roses are red, violets are blue
Cakes are boring, without frosting that is.

Roses are red, violets are blue
Colors are colorful, but not as colorful as you.

Roses are red, violets are blue
x-rays aren't painful, but it's painful to see you think they are.

Roses are red, violets are blue
Pi is not pie, so don't get pi mixed up.

Roses are red, violets are blue
Fish come in many colors, but so do humans.

44.

Silver

Silver looks like the moonlight which falls on my face
Silver sounds like echoing laughter fading into a hallway
bannister
Silver smells like the rusting iron of a dime
Silver tastes like crystallized fruit dipped in sugar
Silver feels like wisdom and old age
Silver reminds me of wishing upon a star.

45.

Red

Red looks like a sailor's sky
Red sounds like sirens
Red smells like fiery chicken wings
Red tastes like Twizzlers
Red feels like basking in the sunshine
Red reminds me of love.

46.

Deep Blue

Deep Blue looks like the endless ocean
Deep Blue sounds like the breath of tides in a timeless dance
Deep Blue smells like calm despair
Deep Blue tastes like the bitter ocean
Deep Blue feels like an empty room echoing
Deep Blue reminds me of ocean's depths where all is lost to
the past.

47.

Pink

Pink looks like flowers
Pink sounds like sweet and cute
Pink smells like Victoria's Secret perfume
Pink tastes like cupcakes with a lot of sprinkles
Pink feels like being cozy after a long day
Pink reminds me of a pig.

48.

Purple

Purple looks like a bowl of grapes
Purple sounds like a monkey in a zoo
Purple smells like a field of lavender
Purple tastes like a juicy grape
Purple feels like slime
Purple reminds me of slime.

49.

Red

Red looks like hate/anger
Red sounds like yelling because how angry I am
Red smells like blood
Red tastes like the salty tears rolling down my face
Red feels like anger
Red reminds me of days I was really mad.

FIVE

Ode to My Favorite Food

Odes are poems that celebrate a special person, place, or thing. This exercise was a wonderful way to get students to write about something they truly love…FOOD! They certainly felt poetic about it and this session enhanced their practice of being grateful for the people, places, and things they have and love.

50.

Ode to Ice Cream

You feel cold on a cold night
You taste sweet but bitter.
You freeze my brain like ice
You aren't very nice for doing that but,
You are still very sweet.

51.

Ode to Ice Cream

You are so creamy and icy
You smell like cotton candy.
You feel like a ripped pillow stuffing,
And you make me happy and you taste so good.

52.

Ode to Blueberries

You pop when broken
In water you're soakin',
Blue as the sky
Without you I'd cry.

I love when you're sour
Give me a big basket, still, I'd never cower,
You're juicy and swell
Oh blueberries I love you well.

53.

Ode to Swedish Meatballs

If you were a person you would be the warmest giver of hugs.
You would inspire people to coat each other in kindness
like your brown gravy.
Because of your different sorts of noodles and juicy meat,
You fill people's bellies and souls with flavors that are
deliciously warm to eat.

54.

Ode to Dark Chocolate

I wake up in the middle of the night
Craving your taste,
Your smooth dark skin
Glistens in the light.

I hasten to feel your bitter
Sweetness against my tongue,
A crack sounds through the silence;
I want to savor you
I slowly bring a piece of you to my mouth,
but my taste buds sing and I
Gobble you down.

I sigh
Is this what ambrosia felt,
Like the Greek gods?

55.

Ode to Ramen

I take my two sticks and pick up the meat
that's engulfed in your chewy and long waves,
You're an old and well-known piece of history.

Each time I bite down
I slurp strands of your angel-like hair;
Your broth is savory but not too salty
and is always my go to meal when I order.

56.

Ode to Pickles

Your shades of Green
Your varied shapes
I love all the faces you take.

Fried, on a sandwich, on a pizza or all on your own
Discs of pure joy, even when you make me pucker
With your briny sensations and garlic overtones filling the air,
an occasional whiff of spice, tanginess and sweetness
Your crunchiness, at times, makes me feel complete.

SIX

Where I'm From
— George Ella Lyon

An important first step in feeling connected to the people and places around us, and more importantly to ourselves, is to realize who and what makes us who we are. In this session the students looked back at their childhoods, delving into themes of identity, home, and history as well as the good and bad times that have all shaped who they are today and who they will continue becoming.

57.

I am from school,
    from teachers & schoolwork.
I am from brick & mortar,
    and desks & pencils.
I am from rain
    whose different array makes me calm.

I am from stone & glass,
    from patience & delay.
I am from secrets & hope
    and from judge & jury.
I am from closet & lock
    from dream & hope.

From #1 but last,
    and from masks.

58.

I am from a little yellow corner store,
    from chalk and muddy shoes.
I am from "get out of there"
    and perfectly planted flowers.
I am from tulips, rose bushes, and chiles
    whose smell intimidates and impresses.

I am from cows and roosters,
    from Garcia and Lopez.
I am from come inside and go wash your hands,
    and from our daily bread and tight ponytails.

I am from Jena and Antonio,
    from tamales and pozole.
From a mezcal maker,
    and from great farmers.

Below the little blossomed tree is the sign that holds the
name of my forever best friends…
I am from those moments, of scraped knees, colorful ice
pops, soft wet grass, and warm fiery embers.

59.

I am from stone walls and smoky kitchens,
　　from stuffed bears and books flung open.
I am from an open courtyard and railings big enough
　　for 5-year-old me to fit through,
　　and from family feeling like foreigners.

I am from lotuses which bloomed from nothing but mud,
　　whose petals fought to see the sunlight.
I am from the corner store where the man would slip me
　　an extra candy when no one was looking,
　　from my family lines, Chugatta and Qureshi.
I am from cover up yourself and don't go alone.

I am from the universe and stardust,
I am from my Nani's strength and my grandfather's tenacity,
　　from street food and mango lassis.
I am from my mom being tricked into giving up her gold,
　　and from my aunt crying for someone to save her,
　　after all it's scary being alone in a place where no one speaks
　　your language, time passing in a blur.

I am from those moments of stepping out into the snow
for the first time, wondering what else
there was to see that I have not yet seen.

60.

I am from Pot and Pans,
    from Crisco and Pressure Cookers.
I am from the swing in the back yard,
Metal, creaking, swinging free.
I am from the Poinciana tree
    whose red flowers decorated our lawn and gave us shade.

I am from a portable hair dryer and a rocking chair,
    from Miki and Tony.
I am from there's a time under the heavens for everything
    and we will cross that bridge when we get there,
I am from bless me father for I have sinned
    and Hail Mary Full of Grace.

I am from Abita and Tia Rosa,
    Café con Leche, white rice and beans.
From the mind my grandmother lost,
    the broken space in my mother's heart.

In my bedroom there was a record player and LPs
    where I played Tapestry by Carole King.
I am from those moments that scared me, pushed me to
be, and live inside of me.

61.

I am from a single mom with three kids,
   from Fabuloso and Vicks.
I am from the heat of the sun burning my skin,
   and chickens running in my backyard.
I am from Coconut Trees
   whose lush green leaves sway gracefully in the breeze
   calling me home.

I am from Dora sippy cups and canicas,
   from Nancy and a missing father.
I am from ponte Vicks and eso es nada,
   from Papa Dios esta belando and Bendicion.
I am from abuela and abuelo,
   from Avena and Kresto,
   from playing Barbie with abuelo
   and from asking my abuela for Avena.

I am from a dozen memories with my family
   from Puerto Rico to Bridgeport.
I am from those moments with real smiles and endless love.

62.

I am from a tiny infinite cobweb playhouse in my
grandmother's backyard,
  from the snack-filled closet that opened with a heavenly
  glow and pristine white unsittable dining room.
I am from Mamita's house—the home where I lived but
never lived in,
  and the home full of all the cousins–friends I could
  want.
I am from the mysterious but plentiful trees,
  whose dropped immature pines fueled my play-time
  potions.

I am from hand painted houses that decorated the
sunroom walls,
  and stacks of PediaSure under the table,
  from Montalvo and Morales
I am from Ay!, si take what you want and come todo,
  from Dios te bendiga and pero que te pasa a ti?
I am from Nereyda and Papá and Grandpa too,
  from limbes and mantecado.
From uprooting our complicated life and roots on the island
and from buying a little house and making a big home.

63.

I am from I n I and Rastafari,
    from dreadlock and St. Mary rocks.
I am from church bells and laughing spells
I am from reggae music whose sound fill yellow bird.

I am from cricket parks and cook outs
    from basement parties and mini marts.
I am from stop chat and na touch dat.

From Jah please and Jesus sees
I am from Eugena and Ena
    from Holidays at Douglas Street and Easter feast.

May trips to Canada, August trips to Jamaica and car rides
    to grandma Gena.
I am from those moments
I n I stand tall and continue to live through it all.

SEVEN

Prompts and Seeds

"Poetry is when an emotion has found its thought and the thought has found words."
— *Robert Frost.*

Writing poetry can be challenging, especially for students attempting it for the first time. In this session the prompts we used inspired the students to feel, think and write. Inspiration for poetry can come from anywhere, but the best inspiration comes from within.

64.

My favorite thing to do is…
Reading books because I like the Baby-sitters Club.
I love it so much.

65.

I feel happy when I play with my sister.
I feel happy when I play Jenga.
I feel happy.

66.

My mom makes me happy.
I'm happy when I'm on the beach.
When my stomach is full with fruit, I'm happy.
I'm happy when I'm around friends
and when my teacher shows me funny pictures.
Today made me happy.

67.

I feel sad because my friend said
that he's not going to my party, forever.
My birthday is May 8th.
I want all my six friends, five girls and one boy to be there.

68.

I feel happy when I get money.
I feel happy when I get 100$.
I feel happy when I have a smoothie.
I feel happy when I drink cold water.
I feel happy when I get paid.
I feel happy when I have a lot of money.
I feel happy when I gain money.
I feel happy when someone gives me money.
I feel happy when money comes my way.
I feel happy when I find 80,000 $ on the ground.
I feel happy when I get a lot of US Currency.
I feel the most happy with money.

69.

Nothing

I don't have a favorite thing about myself.
I never cared to pay attention to things about me to notice
a favorite.
Growing up I was always told opposites of what I should
hear,
"You're ugly, I hate you."
I never cared because if I think highly of myself,
then that's all that matters, right? Wrong.
Not liking anything about yourself is hard,
but others not liking you is even harder.
I know I have potential to find that favorite thing, but I
also know
that it'll be a while till I find that day.
Hopefully that day can be soon.

70.

My favorite thing about myself is
The way that I care no matter the stare.
I think big and broad, although I'm not tall.
I'm average height, but not afraid to reach new heights.
I love that I take naps 6 hours long.
I hang on to each word you may say, so you know I'm connected,
That I like to be moment to moment,
So I don't get disconnected.
These are a few of my favorite things that my life brings.

71.

My favorite thing about myself is what sets me apart.
It's taken a few years to find it, and it was a pretty rough start.
But I love my individuality, the unique beat of my heart.

I am who I am, like no one yet to be seen.
Short, eyes brown and hair that is green.
A weird, unique girl since I was 13.

My interest diverse, and boy there's a lot.
My playlist goes Disney, BTS, worship and even some rock.
From America, some ASL, Spanish and chotto wa nihongo wa
wakarimasu ("I understand a bit of Japanese")

I'll eat through books yet wish they would last.
Minecraft for hours, till the day has gone and passed.
Keep Christ in my heart, but love rocking my bats.

My favorite thing about myself is what sets me apart.
It's taken a few years to find it, and it was a pretty rough start.
But I love my individuality, the unique beat of my heart.

72.

My Authenticity

My favorite thing about myself is my authenticity.
I see the world for how it is,
I see people for who they are,
I understand we are all unique,
I see the beauty in everyone I meet,
even if I'm afraid of them for how they speak.

To tell the truth is what I believe,
no matter if some hearts will erupt,
for then I know a change will come.

My authenticity is clear as a crystal, shining so bright!
My authenticity is tough as leather and I've weathered the
lessons.
My authenticity is the gateway to now, where I live in
gratitude and love.

EIGHT

Renga

Closing the sessions with Renga, a 700-year-old Japanese poetic form that encourages the collaborative composition of poems, was the perfect culmination to the poetry workshop. We opened with Giving, we closed with Giving, coming full circle.

These beautifully written linked poems are an acknowledgment of the HEAL program's contribution to "community" and belief in "self," and promote examples of **Health, Empathy, Altruism, and Love**, HEAL's philosophy of *healing* through service to others.

These Renga community poems were also recorded by the children and volunteers in the Verso Studio at The Westport Library. You can hear the *Voices of our Children* on the Youth and Young Adults HwH website.

Westport, CT Schools

73.

Giving is something we do
to help others like me and you.
When I give my friend a hug
Giving makes me feel really happy
and a little sad if they don't like it.

Giving makes me feel good
because I like helping other people.
I don't have a lot of money
but I can give my friendship and love.
I give a gift to my mom… she feels happy.
And I hug my mom and I was happy.

Giving feelings so your friend knows how you feel.
And the friends like when you tell them how you feel.
Give feelings to other people that like you and be kind.
Giving makes me feel great
because you know the other people feel gorgeous!

I could give kindness and love to those in need.
Once I give I feel complete.
Once I receive I feel no mean.
I like when people get kind to me
Because I feel so relaxed and kind back!

When I give I feel joyful to give back.
When I receive I feel happy.
(and when I get money!)
I feel good when I give keychains.
They give to us. We give to them. We all give together.

Norwalk, CT Schools

74.

Giving is magical like the stars at night! They remind me of,
lighting up a pathway that'll lead me to my fate.
I give all the love I have to offer and hope for a small amount
back.
Feeling like a little mouse, in a large cornfield,
I always go back to look at the stars.
How beautiful, how insignificant those stars are, as am I.
Are they looking up at me, twinkling too?

To me giving means letting go, letting go of myself
in the pursuit of helping others because sometimes,
giving is all I do.
Like an endless ocean, I give in different ways.
Sometimes I give like rain, pouring down, overbearing
but the possibility of a rainbow appearing keeps me giving.

Somewhere over the rainbow dreams can come true
Giving me the warmth of the sun, having fun,
showing me to feel, got be real.
The rainbow is so colorful and bright, but it's leaving our sight.
It's coming to an end.
Now what shall I see while I stare at the blue sky?

Like a little mouse in a large cornfield, when all I know is
lost, I long for more.

Though I know, with how lonely I feel, I'm never alone;
The stars will always be there, even when I can't see them,
giving me company.

I feel at home, I snuggle in the hay and let the love in my heart
keep me warm and I drift to sleep.
I dream of what I was and what I can be.
The possibilities filling me with determination.
I don't know where I'm going but I have a dream
and I lay here waiting for the morning sun.

The sun that might not shine as bright
but still fills me with a lot of love to give.
I wish I can do more but now I have to move on,
to move on with the sky that tells a story every waking day.
And to learn how to forgive myself, for my loyalty is too big.

Forgiveness is hard. But holding on pulls you back.
Giving and living makes me whole.
The stress gets freed, and I can live a lot longer.
My heart beats to the wind while the sun shines down.
I love to give, but all I cannot, for I need me.

Giving and loving is essential for sustaining life.
Love is necessary for life.
Life is Love.

Wilton, CT Schools

75.

Giving is magical like the stars at night!
They remind me of the moments of my life.
The highways and byways turn so fast,
I try to hold on, I must go on.
Giving is essential and I will always remember,
I must go on to give to the world.
Giving is a way to make sure you don't become stingy.

Giving to the world propels us like a car on the road.
It helps us to move forward and watch the trees
and change of seasons go by.
The seasons change and so do I,
giving me a sense of purpose and humility.
Moving forward with each season gives me a sense of
renewal and awe for the new chapter of life unfolding.
Life like the seasons is full of changes and new beginnings.

Like a newborn baby we welcome to the world,
so soft and sweet, needing only love and milk.
As they grow so do their needs,
they amaze us with their wonder and free spirits!
As toddlers running and climbing the mighty oak trees.
They climb and climb, they have no worries in the world,
yet they cry about the smallest things.
A child's imagination knows no bounds;
maybe that is why we always wish to return back to it.

Returning to our imaginations gives us a mindful
awareness of ourselves. Allows us to wonder
how do we help ourselves and assist others with their free-
spirited passions. Passions that help everyone relax and
calm down.
Passion helps us give and love.
Passion helps us grow.

Bridgeport, CT Schools

76.

Giving is magical like the stars at night!
They remind me of,
the way people love each other,
Gifting things to each other like magpies.
In giving we find joy's embrace,
hearts open wide, a selfless grace.
Giving is the embrace that replenishes the heart with love,
Keeping the cycle of love, life, and laughter afloat.

Keeping laughter afloat smiles all through the room,
full of love and lust, until it all dies, yet this isn't goodbye.
New flowers bloom with the glow of the new moon,
We give small pieces that give us new leases
on the lives we live, so we must strive to give.
Boundless spirited energy sparkling,
rays of hope sounds of love.

A star's light—boundless energy eternal, is a lingering
spark or death.
The act of giving too, has a physical end.
Though it lives on forever as a light and love passed on
eternally,
long outliving us all!

About the Editors

jennifer lyn amon is a passionate program director/developer with twenty years of experience in the human services field providing group and mentoring support to underserved youth and individuals throughout Fairfield County. Creator of programming and curriculums for non-profit and community service organizations using strength-based approaches and methodologies that create a sense of belonging and build self-confidence. Organizer of community-based events providing volunteer opportunities connecting individuals to a greater good.

Sylvie Middleton is a Miami native, poet, and life coach living in the New York City Metropolitan Area. She is the author of a collection of poems, "*The Year That Was, Immersed in Poetry.*" What started as a personal outlet in her youth transitioned into a poetic journey of transformation that inspired the creation of a program that provides others with the opportunity to follow her path to healing, (PoeticTransformation™).

In the summer of 2022 while working as a volunteer with Homes with Hope, Sylvie created a poetry workshop for the Youth Services HEAL Program. The success of this course led to the creation of this poetry book, *Voices of Our Children*.

Sylvie continues to write, believing in the power of words and their magic to empower, enlighten and enrich the human spirit.

EXPRESS YOURSELF HERE

EXPRESS YOURSELF HERE

EXPRESS YOURSELF HERE

EXPRESS YOURSELF HERE

EXPRESS YOURSELF HERE